they need to become famous.

Is Just Around the Corner

promise

Star   Elegance

BUY
THIS

FIFTY

into the Spotlight

Star

the

zilly

A Modern-Day Fable by Kelly Parks Snider

GOATHOUSE PRESS

MADISON WISCONSIN

The illustrations for this book were created using acrylic paint, crayons, rubber stamps, oil pastels, and collage on paper bags
The text and display type were set in Minion Pro
Composed in the United States of America
Designed by Zucker Design
Edited by Aimee Jackson

Printed and bound in the United States of America
Second Edition
10 9 8 7 6 5 4 3 2 1

To my parents.

Thank you for always
encouraging me
to scribble outside
the lines.

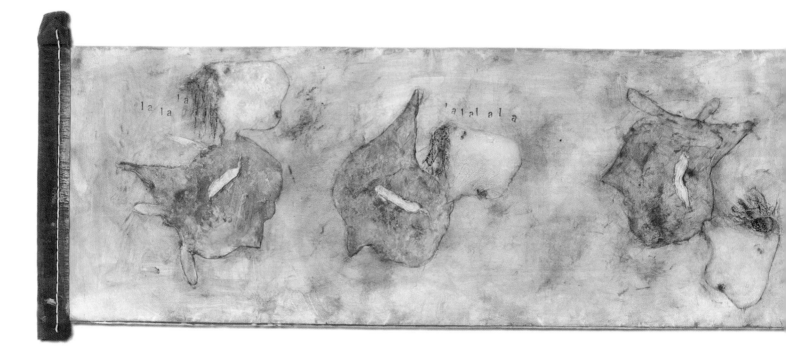

Once upon a modern time there flew an
out-of-the-ordinary flyer named Zilly.

Zilly loved soaring through the gusty sky. Around and around, up and down she would fly.

Zilly loved the humming hums that filled the air and how each flippity flight tickled her tummy with delight.

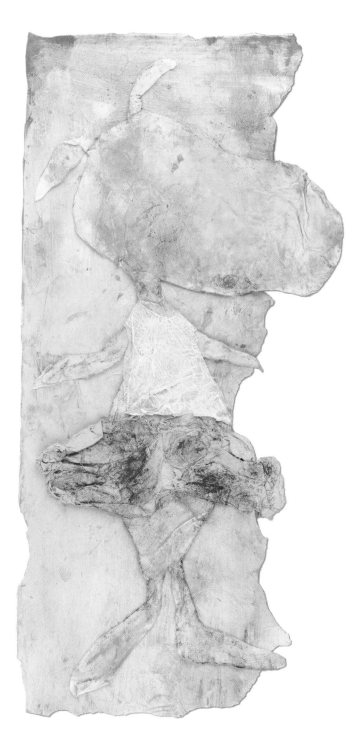

Zilly's best friend was a
little goat named Mingle.

"Mingle is magnificent,"
Zilly would say. "She likes
what she likes, and she
really likes me!"

One gusty day while zipping around as Zilly loved to do, she overheard grumbles and rude shouts.

"Look at Zilly. She doesn't fly straight like us," snipped a smug flyer.

"She is too bumpy!" snarled another.

"Blah. Too many flops!" booed a third.

Zilly was stunned.

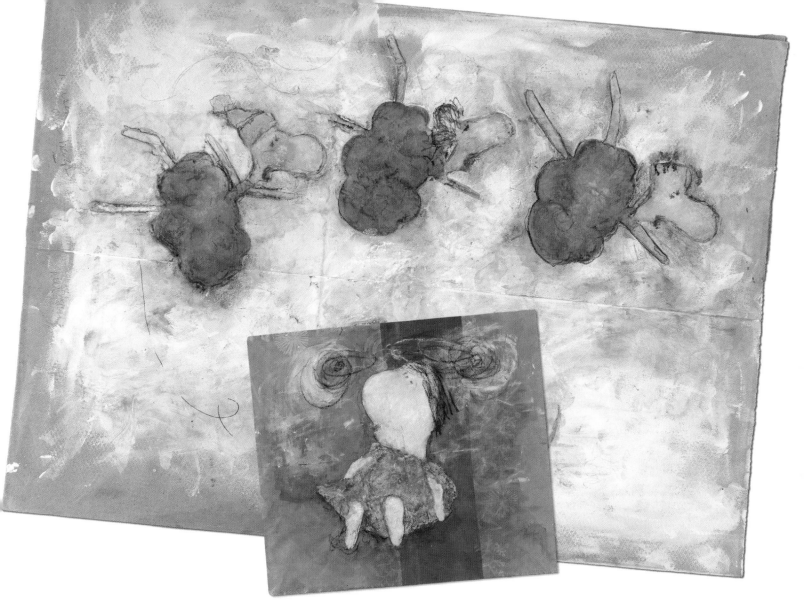

She drooped and then she dropped and then her flippity flip turned into an embarrassing flop.

Flustered and not knowing what to do, Zilly grabbed Mingle's hoof and off they flew!

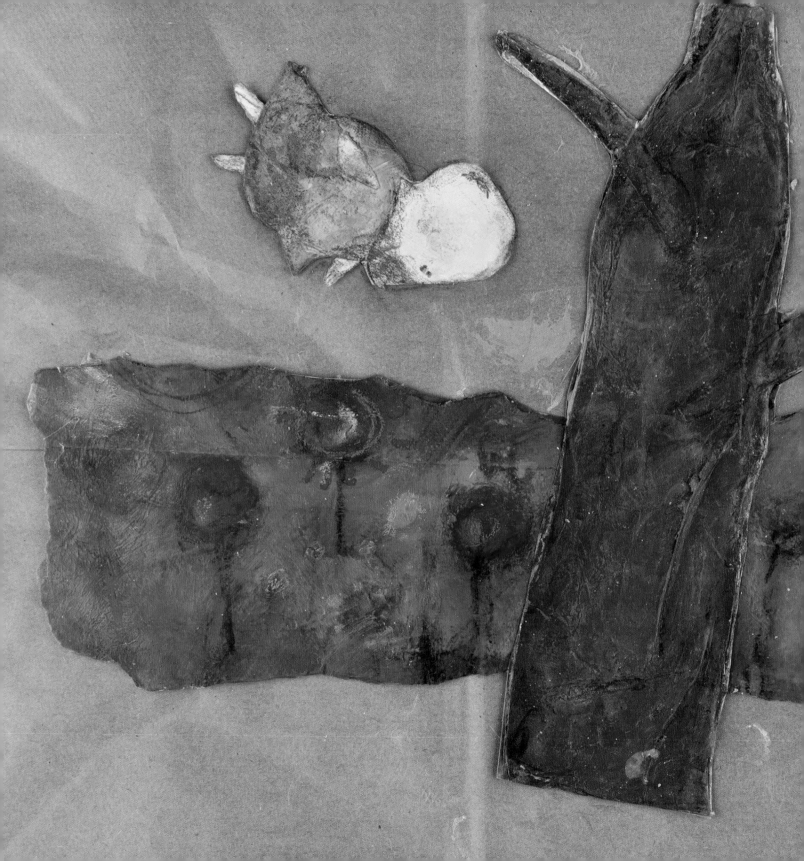

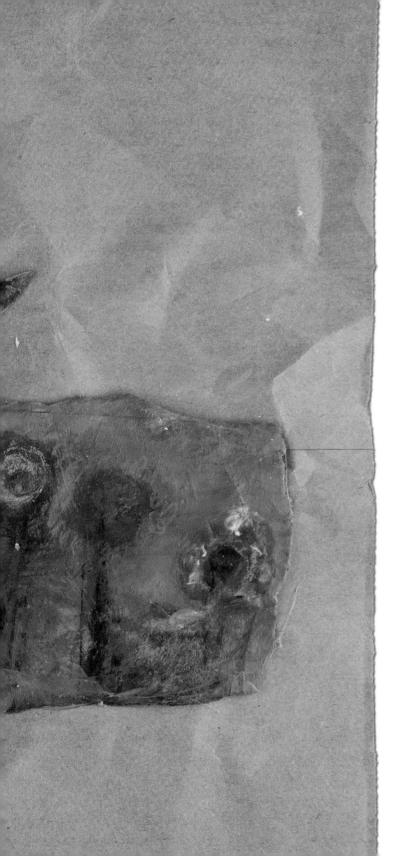

Zilly and Mingle spent the rest of the day wandering through the sky. They flew upside down and sometimes sideways.

"What the other flyers say is not true!" Mingle said. "Don't let them make you feel bad about being you."

Zilly and Mingle stumbled upon a gigantic billboard.

"Sign up today!" it read. "Flying lessons for flyers who want to fit in."

The billboard promised that all flying lessons came complete with a nifty look-alike outfit, a book of easy-to-memorize flying routines, and a sparkly award.

Out-of-the-ordinary types were not invited. Flips, zips, and bumpiness were banned. And goats were not allowed.

"Oh, dear," Zilly said to herself.

Zilly gazed at the billboard and she gazed some more.
Fitting in seemed so fashionable. And a nifty outfit seemed
almost necessary. And who wouldn't want a sparkly award?

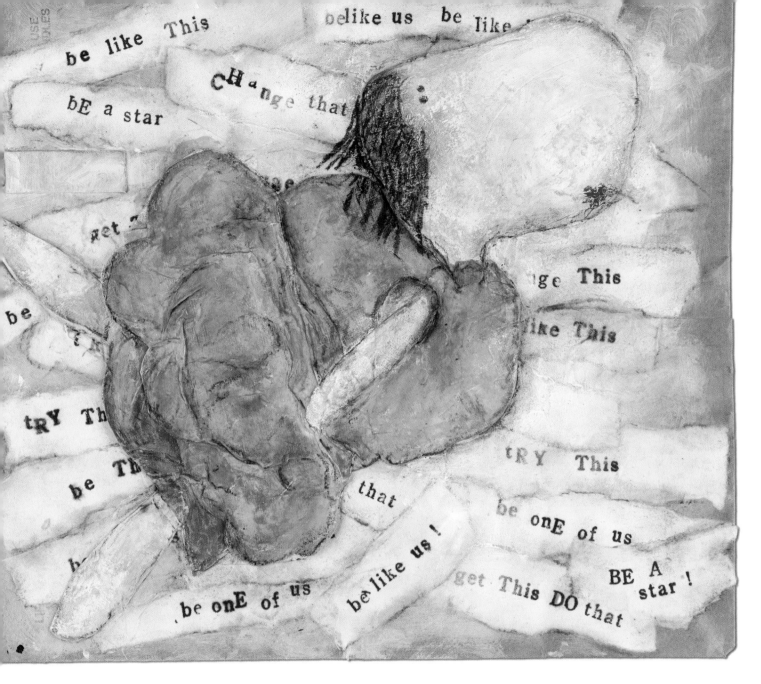

"This is it!" Zilly exclaimed. "If beautiful means being like all of you, then that is what I will do!"

"That billboard is not true!" Mingle said. "It's trying to trick you into being someone who isn't really you!"

It was too late. Zilly had signed on the dotted line and announced it to the other flyers.

"And I do not know that goat!"

Mingle looked away and proudly declared, "There is nothing wrong with me. I like being me, and I am the way I am supposed to be!"

Zilly practiced her new routine,
and she practiced it some more.

The big day arrived! No smiling sounds could be heard anywhere.

"She doesn't fit in," snipped a smug flyer.

"She is still too bumpy," giggled another.

"Blah. Who invited her?" boomed a third.

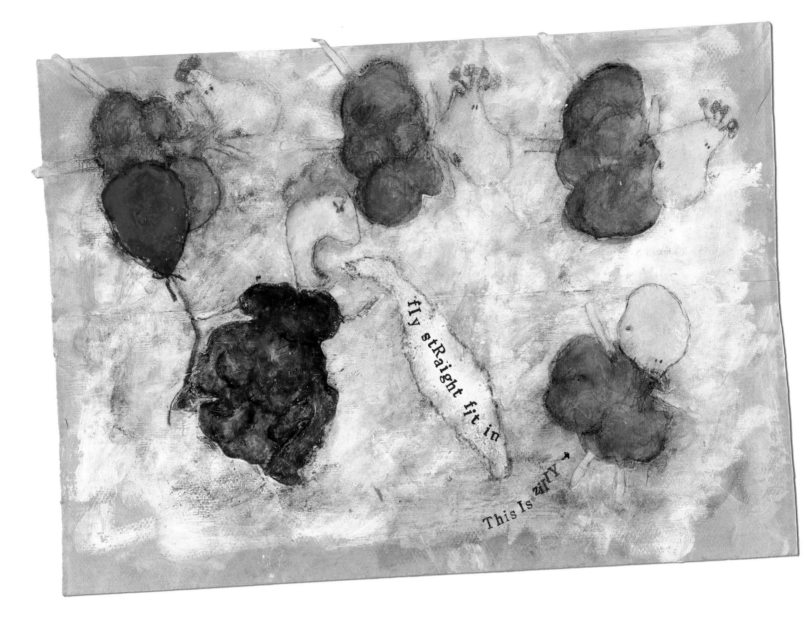

With her most determined nod, Zilly made a leap up into
the very serious sky.

Zilly tried flying straight. Zilly tried flying orderly.
But instead, she zipped out of formation. Zilly whooped and she
ooped and then she blasted into a furious flyer, who banged into a
bumbling bragger. "Pardon me!" "Oops." "So sorry." "Didn't mean
to." Zilly kindly and continuously apologized.

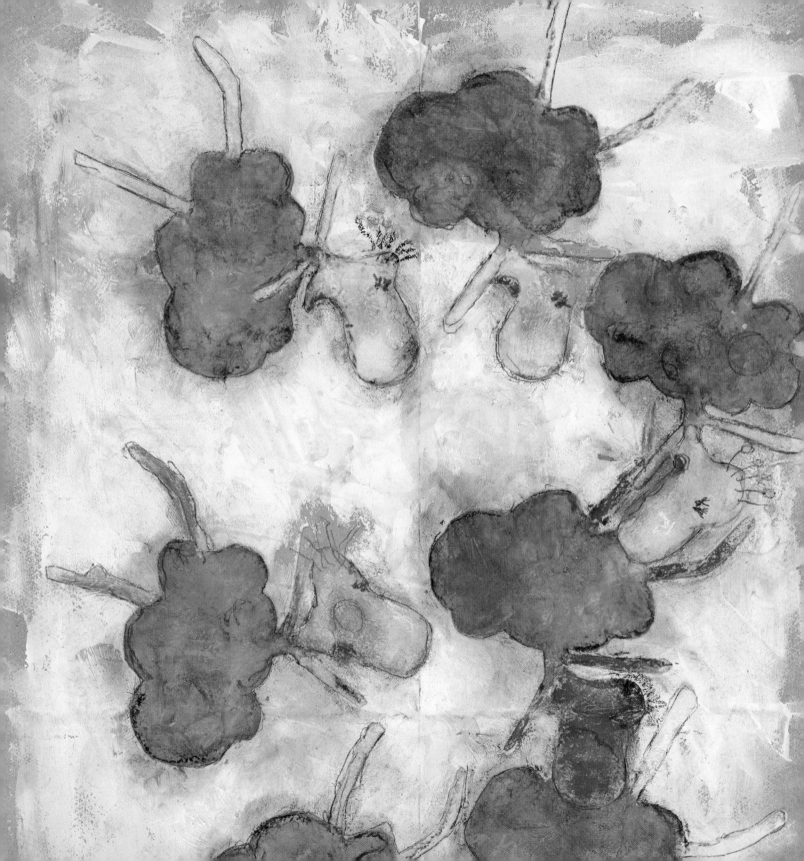

What followed next was an enormous ruckus that sent all the angry-faced flyers tumbling down and down!

Wishing she could hide, Zilly flew up and around and away from the other flyers, whispering to herself, "Oh, terribleness."

As she flew away, Zilly
heard a friendly cheer.

"Hooray for Zilly!"

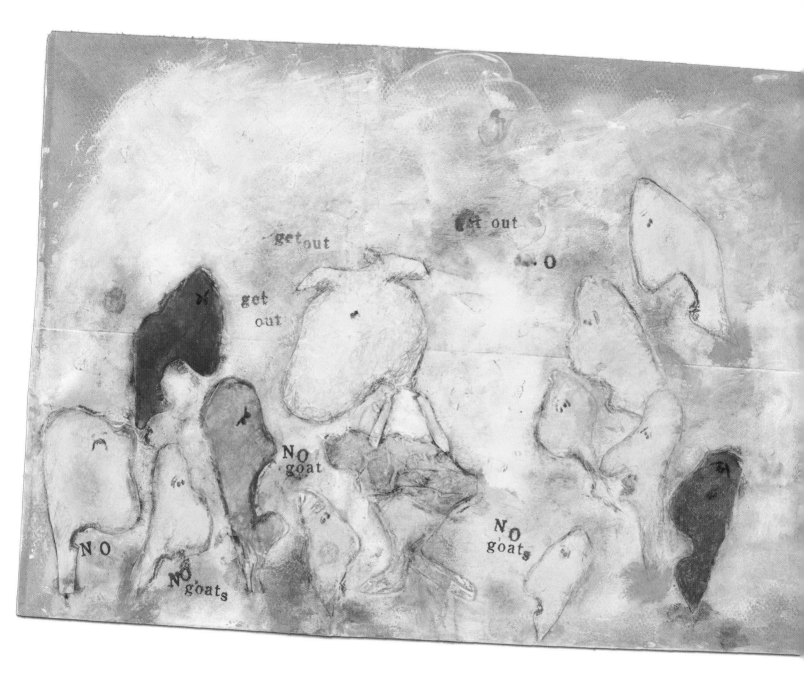

Zilly looked down. She could hardly believe her eyes. An angry crowd had gathered, and trembling in the middle was Mingle.

Zilly had to do something! Ever so swiftly she blasted past the frowning flyers and turned up her nose at their stinging stares.

With an amazingly daring dip, Zilly reached down and snatched her faithful friend, and off they flew, away from the rumbles and grumbles below.

Zilly soared above the crowd and proudly declared, "You can't change me! I like being me, and I am exactly the way I am supposed to be!"

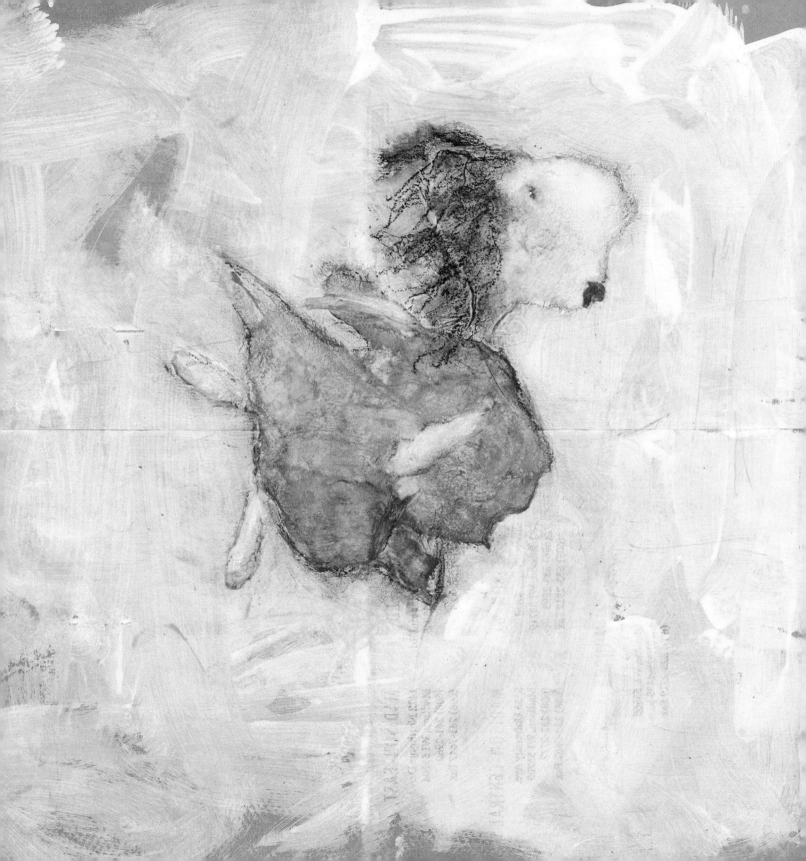

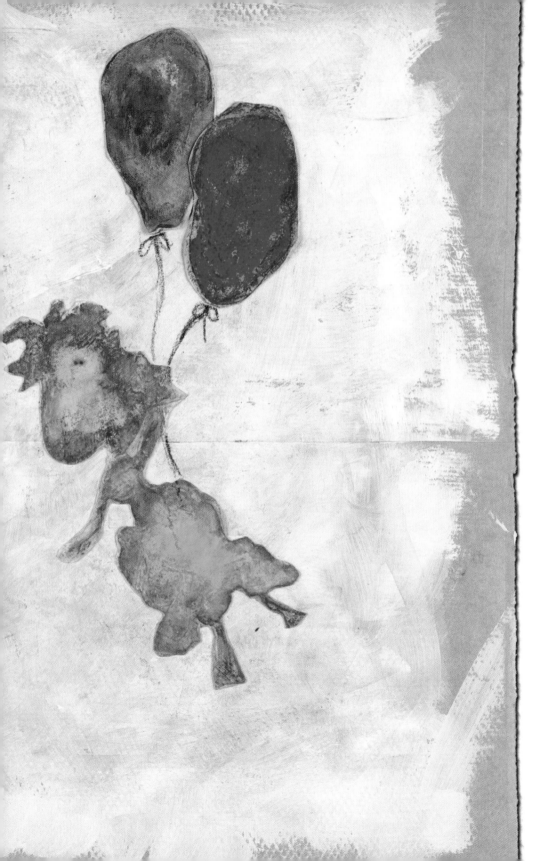

And from
that moment
forward all the
rules changed.

- Love yourself just the way you are.
- Be a true original (like Zilly).
- Focus on the things that make you unique and special.
- Pay less attention to magazine advertisements and commercials.
- Stop comparing yourself to others.
- Be your own trendsetter.
- Devote your time to doing the activities that truly bring you happiness.
- Take care of yourself.
- Voice your opinions.
- Spread kindness to the world.
- Be a role model.
- Always be nice to goats.

NEW RULES

1. Flips that flop are fabUloUs.

2. Unique flying performers are fashionable.

3. Goats are glamorous.

4. Bumpiness is always beautiful.

For more information, visit zillybook.com, projectgirl.org, and these other valuable resources:

zillybook.com
projectgirl.org
hardygirlshealthywomen.org
commercialfreechildhood.org
newdream.org
commonsensemedia.org
freepress.net
newmoon.com
amightygirl.com

AUTHOR'S NOTE

ZiLLY is my protest book. Like Zilly, I have been influenced by the false claims, lies, and promises in advertisements. The landscape of today's popular culture is cluttered with ads and media messages that tell our children, time and again, to follow a path that leads to conformity, competition, and awards rather than following their passions. This steady barrage of messages leaves all of us feeling pressured, anxious, and empty.

Zilly's story provides children and caring adults with a springboard to introduce thoughtful discussions about the influence of media on our lives.

Zilly is the story of a wonderfully out-of-the-ordinary flyer who strives to fit in. Wanting acceptance from the conforming crowd around her, Zilly tries to hide the quirky and spontaneous qualities that define her individuality. Mirroring kid culture, a billboard encourages Zilly to join a school for flyers who want to fit in, a place that allows little room for self-expression and creativity. Signing up means that Zilly will lose touch with her originality. By the end of the story, the closed and competitive culture transforms into one of cooperation, acceptance, and collaboration. Zilly and the other flyers celebrate their own uniqueness and the uniqueness of others.

DISCUSSION QUESTIONS

Who is Zilly? What does Zilly love to do? What do you love to do? Zilly loves to fly because it delights her. She doesn't fly to win. She flies because of the joy it brings to her life, and eventually she realizes that her uniqueness brings joy to others.

Who is Mingle? Would you like to be friends with Mingle? Why or why not? Is Mingle a good friend? Is Zilly always a good friend? Why or why not? Are the other flyers Zilly's friends? Why or why not? What makes you a good friend?

Zilly becomes influenced by the other flyers and a billboard. Do you ever feel pressure to change who you are? How does this pressure make you feel?

What is media? Where do you see it? TV, radio, internet, magazines, newspapers, books, music, video games, billboards, signs, labels. Media is everywhere. We can't escape it. We are all influenced by advertising to some degree.

Have you ever bought something or changed something about you because of promises made in an ad? Were you ever disappointed with what the product did for you? Advertisements try to make us believe that we need to buy things to make us happy and to solve our problems. Advertisements confuse us. They try to make us feel that we aren't good enough so that we keep buying their products. Going to the mall and buying and buying and buying doesn't change anything about who we really are or solve our problems. It only changes how we look on the outside.

Who can solve your problems? You are the only one who can solve your own problems, but you can get help from people you trust.

Who may be able to help you solve your problems? Parents, friends, teachers.

Why do you think the pictures were made on paper bags? How do the pictures make you feel? Is it important to reuse things and take care of our environment? What kinds of things do you do to take care of your world?

Children's books are powerful. With words and art, we create an away space for children. There seems to be very few spaces in our children's lives where they can experience stillness. Good art and great books can open our eyes to new ways of seeing this world.

Kelly lives on a little farm outside of Madison, Wisconsin, with her family and zillions of pets, including a little goat named Mingle.

Kelly is the co-founder of Project Girl (www.projectgirl.org), a national program that combines art, media literacy, and youth-led activism.

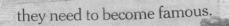they need to become famous.

Is Just Around the Corner.

promise

Star

Elegance

BUY THIS

FIFTY

ato the Spotlight

Star